Peter is moving house today.
He lies on his bedroom floor one last time.
All the furniture has gone!

3

He watches the removal men.
They hurry to and fro like ants,
carrying boxes.

4

Leave alone!

First published in this edition in 2010 by Evans Brothers Ltd
2A Portman Mansions
Chiltern Street
London W1U 6NR

This edition © Evans Brothers Limited 2010
© Van In, Lier, 1995. Van In Publishers, Grote Markt 39, 2500 Lier, Belgium

Originally published in Belgium as Altijd moeten ze mij hebben

British Library Cataloguing in Publication Data

Bode, Ann de.
    Leave me alone!. -- (Side by side)
    1. Bullying--Juvenile fiction. 2. Schools--Juvenile
    fiction. 3. Children's stories.
    I. Title II. Series
    839.3'1364-dc22

ISBN-13: 9780237543082

Printed in China

Peter's already said goodbye to his best friend Simon.
He's really going to miss him.

'Are we nearly there yet?' asks Peter.
It's a long way in the car.

The new house is really big, like a castle!
Peter can see his bedroom window,
right at the top.

Time for lunch! The furniture is still in the van, so they eat sandwiches on the floor. This is fun! thinks Peter.

The removal men carry the boxes into the house. Peter can't wait to get into his new room.

Before Peter unpacks, he wants
to show Tiger his new room.
But where is he?
What a mess!

Finally, Peter opens the last box.
There he is!

Peter goes downstairs for tea.
'Have you unpacked yet?' asks Mum.
'Um, not yet,' he mumbles.

'Why don't you go outside for a
bit?' says Mum.
As he walks down the road Peter
bumps into a boy with spiky hair.
He looks like a hedgehog. And
he's not very friendly.

'Look where you're going,' he says.
He grabs Tiger, and stamps all over him.
Poor Tiger!

The next day Peter starts at his new school. He doesn't know the answer to any of the sums. He feels stupid.

The boy in front laughs at him.
Look who it is! Hedgehog boy!

At breaktime the boy comes up to Peter.
'Why can't you do the sums? We learnt them ages ago,' he says.
Then he punches Peter and walks off.

17

After that everyone picks on Peter.
Leave me alone! he thinks.

Jack, the boy with spiky hair, is worst.
Peter's scared of him. He's lonely
without any friends.

But in his dreams Peter is happy.
He dreams that Tiger is a giant.
He chases Jack.

20

Tiger roars like thunder.
Jack's so scared he wets himself.

But when Peter wakes up
he realises he's wet the bed.
Oh no! He starts to change the sheets.

Mum comes in and helps him.
'What's wrong, Peter?'
Peter tells her everything. He
feels much better.

Peter's teacher tries to help him.
'You must tell me if anyone
bullies you,' she says.
Peter stops getting bullied at school.
But Jack still picks on him after school.

One day, Jack is ill and doesn't come to school. Peter hopes Jack will be ill for a long time!

Mum has an idea. 'Let's have
a party!' she says.
Peter invites everyone. Even Jack.

Peter takes the invitation to Jack's house because he's still ill.
Mum shows him the way.

'I'm glad you've come,' says Jack's mum.
'No one ever comes to play with Jack.'

Jack's in bed, covered with spots.
He looks sad, not scary.
His room's full of cuddly toys –
just like Peter's!

Peter sits on the bed.
It rustles – Jack's got a plastic sheet!
Jack goes bright red.

Jack and Peter aren't so
different after all!
Jack shows him his stamp book.
He's really friendly.

It's party day! Everyone comes.
Jack even brings a present – a new Tiger!
Peter feels happier than he's been
for a long time.